CIRCUS
April 1st

Contents

6:00 A.M. *The Circus Comes to Tannersville*

ON the first day of April the Circus came to Tannersville. Early spring mornings in Tannersville (since it is a sea-coast town) are usually dark and murky with fog. But this particular morning was exceptionally dark. As the engineer said when he pulled his throttle and brought the circus train to a stop, "This is the darkest morning yet. You can't see the back of your hand."

It was very difficult to unload the circus cars. The floodlights that usually lit up the railroad siding could not pierce the fog. The heavy gilded wagons that held the cages of

1

the wild lion, the tiger, the polar bear and the wild (but timid) monkeys were rolled off the flat cars as everybody shouted to everybody else, "Watch what you are doing."

There was a dark exciting confusion and noise all along the railroad siding where the circus train had stopped. But in the big freight car that held the best . . . the most important act . . . the Grand Finale Act of the circus . . . it was quiet.

Every year the Barton and Carlin Circus had its regular number of funny clowns, wild animals, acrobats, dancing horses and performing seals. And every year there was one especially wonderful act they kept as a surprise for the Grand Finale.

This year the B. & C. Circus was proud to present Jo, Um and Bo. They were the Elephant Triplets (Jo-Um-Bo . . . do you get it? That's the name Jumbo cut up into three names . . . Jo-Um-Bo.) That was Mr. Carlin's idea to name them Jo, Um and Bo. Of course, that's not the proper way to spell Jumbo. But since everyone knows Jumbo stands for elephant Mr. Carlin thought that by just printing on the circus posters "The Magnificent Jo, Um and Bo, The Most Wonderful Act in the World," no one could possibly guess that the special surprise Grand Finale act was an elephant act.

Now this is what made Jo, Um and Bo's act so special.

2

They each were painted with rather largish red, white and blue stripes. Their heads and front legs were all red. Their middle sections a broad white stripe and their hind legs, hips and tails were all blue!

The act began when they came into the big arena (after the chariot races) walking on their hind legs and waving small American flags held high in their trunks while the band played "Three cheers for the Red, White and Blue." It was a very impressive sight.

Then they danced (the waltz and other dances), played baseball, and did other tricks and finally marched out of the arena walking again on their blue hind legs swaying their white middles and with their red heads held high as they proudly waved their little flags in a blaze of spotlights and glory.

Young Danny Morgan climbed out of his bunk in one of the sleeping cars of the circus train and stumbled out into the chilly fog. He walked back to the freight car in which Jo, Um and Bo travelled. It was young Danny's job to spray the red, white and blue colors on Jo, Um and Bo every morning before the circus parade and every night with a hose and warm water he washed them down.

Danny was the assistant elephant man. He was a gentle, tow-headed boy about sixteen years old. Danny had helped

Mr. Carlin, who had been a first-class elephant man before he bought a half interest in the B. & C. Circus, to train the elephants. But now that Mr. Carlin had attained the dignity of owning half a circus he couldn't be seen in public associating only with elephants. Mr. Carlin thought that might show favoritism and the others in the circus might feel neglected. He usually bounded around all over the circus with a pleasant smile for everyone, a cheery hello, a handshake or a pat on the back . . . but when he came to the elephants he always lingered a little longer. He always gave them a special pat and usually he gave young Danny a special bit of instruction on elephant care (out of the side if his mouth) as he went by.

Mr. Barton, the tall thin partner of the Barton and Carlin Circus, just took care of the money. He took care of it as it came in through the ticket windows and took care of it as it went out for wages, bills for hay, ham and eggs, spangles, new cages and whatever anyone buys to keep a circus going.

Young Danny stumbled back through the confusion of the awakened circus train to get to his elephants. All along the way he kept bumping into people and stumbling over the railroad ties in the darkness. He said, "Excuse me," over and over again. Sometimes people said, "Sure," or

4

"Watch your step, kid." When he bumped into the camels they did not say anything.

Finally, he reached the elephants' freight car. He pulled open the big sliding door, climbed aboard and pulled the door shut after him. The one electric bulb lit up the inside of the big freight car with a warm yellow glow. The eyes of Jo, Um and Bo all turned to watch Danny as he moved about the car. They peacefully went on chewing their breakfast. Danny gave each a pat on the trunk, said "Good morning" and went to work.

First thing . . . with an old sugar scoop he scooped up some dry white color from a barrel and dumped it into a large pail. Then from another barrel he scooped up some red color and threw that into a second pail and finally, he scooped some dry blue color into a third pail. Then he hosed some water into the three pails and mixed each of the pails with three long sticks. That's the way he always mixed the red, white and blue colors. After the colors were well mixed Danny stuck the cylinder of a suction pump into the white paint, clamped it to the pail and began pumping the white paint out through the long thin rubber tube that he held in his other hand. It was just like using an old-fashioned bicycle pump . . . but instead of pumping out air, Danny pumped out paint.

The paint came out in a thin spray and while the elephants went on rhythmically chewing their hay breakfast Danny sprayed a broad white stripe on Jo, then Um, and at last on Bo. He was the smallest of the three and he was always the easiest to get covered with paint so Danny always sprayed him last.

Then Danny pumped and sprayed some blue paint on the back ends of the three elephants. They gently swung their tails and twitched their heavy hides a little but they all stood still until Danny had finished spraying on the blue paint. Now came the only unpleasant part for everyone . . . spraying the red paint on their forelegs and their heads . . . particularly their heads.

The elephants had been trained to close their eyes and mouths and to stop breathing for a moment as the red paint was sprayed on their heads. But sometimes they forgot and they opened their mouths or breathed a little or peeped with one eye as Danny sprayed the red . . . especially Bo. And often Bo had red paint squirted right into his eye. But it was not a poisonous paint (just a casein paint which is made of dried milk with some vegetable coloring) and although it was a little unpleasant to have some paint and water squirted into your eye . . . none of the elephants made a fuss about it. He who had been squirted (and it was usually Bo) would just blink, shut his eyes tighter and look sort of ashamed that he had forgotten his training.

6

When the elephants were all sprayed Red, White and
Blue and the paint dried, Danny pulled the big freight car
door open, stuck his head out into the dark of the morning
and shouted, "Ready here!"

A crew of roustabouts (that's what they call circus
laborers) came along in a few minutes and arranged a big,
heavy gangplank from the freight car door to the ground.
And led by Danny, Jo, Um and Bo, looking very handsome
in their fresh coats of paint, ponderously walked down
the gangplank to the ground.

One of the roustabouts who was known for his wit suddenly slapped his own forehead. Everyone recognized that

7

signal. It meant he was going to tell a joke so everyone stopped doing what they were doing and waited.

"Hey, Danny," he cried, "what's this? You've painted your elephants orange, white and blue! It's the Dutch flag! Since when did these big fellows become Dutchmen. . . ."

Danny blushed and looked closely at the red painted heads of Jo, Um and Bo. They looked red to him . . . but in that bad light he might have mixed some yellow color in with the red . . . and maybe it was orange.

"Look's red to me," said Danny.

"Nope! It's orange!" said the witty roustabout.

"Might be . . . Do they look orange to you?" asked Danny turning to the other roustabouts.

They all grinned broadly. The witty roustabout slapped him on the shoulder.

"Naw. They're not orange. . . . They're red all right, Danny boy. Do you know what day it is? It's April Fool's Day!" And he slapped Danny good-naturedly again.

Danny grinned with relief.

"You're a good sport, Danny, my boy. You can take a joke. Now remember, this is April Fool's Day. Don't take any wooden nickels."

Just then Mr. Carlin came bustling along.

"Morning, Danny," he said. "Morning, everybody . . ."

Everybody said, "Good morning" or "Hi boss." The elephants waved their trunks gently.

"Danny," said Mr. Carlin, "we're setting up the tents in the big meadow on the other side of town. We'll be marching right through the streets. Jo, Um and Bo will make up the vanguard . . . the end of our friendly little circus army . . . so trail right along after the camels and don't lose sight of them. There are some swamp bogs alongside the road. We'd lose us an elephant if one of these babies got off the road in this fog. Be careful, Danny. . . . Oh, oh, the wagons are rolling!"

And Mr. Carlin ran off blowing the whistle that hung from a cord around his neck. He had forgotten to give the man driving the first gilded wagon (the one with the lion's cage) some instruction . . .

"Yes, sir," said Danny to Mr. Carlin's fast disappearing back. And then he turned to the elephants and said, "All right, fellers, line up!"

Jo moved forward and stood in front of Um. Um quietly curled his red trunk around Jo's dangling blue tail. Then Bo moved around and reached for Jo's tail with his trunk. He held it lightly.

7:00 A.M. *Bo Loses the Circus*

TANNERSVILLE is a small town but it boasts two railroad stations. There is the East railroad station where the trains stop that go north and south along the coast. And then there is the West railroad station where the trains go east and west going to and coming from the western states, the Great Plains and the Rocky Mountains. The circus train had come in on the eastern railroad track and the march of the circus people and animals had to cross the western railroad tracks to get to the big meadow where Mr. Carlin said they planned to put up their tent.

It so happened that just as the first heavy gilded wagon reached the western railroad tracks . . . the cross-bars

11

were let down. A long train of freight cars was coming in from the west. The march of the circus people and the animals was stopped.

Danny, Jo, Um and Bo at the end of the line waited patiently for the freight train to pass by. They heard the chugging of the engine that pulled the train, then they heard the rumbling clackity-clack of the freight car wheels but they could not see the train from where they stood. They were so far away from the railroad crossing.

The elephants stood quietly holding tails with trunks. Bo who was at the very end and held Um's tail (although no one held his) had stopped under a large willow tree. The long slender branches came down around his head and dropped little rivulets of water on him. The distant rumbling of the freight car wheels made Bo sleepy. He closed his eyes for a moment. His head began to nod and his trunk which he kept gently curled around Um's tail slowly uncurled. For a moment he lost Um's tail and with his eyes still closed he reached around in the darkness to find it again. Then he let himself fall fast asleep.

Bo awoke with a start. He found the fog had lifted a little. And in the pearly grey morning light he suddenly realized he was alone. The circus had gone on without him. And he discovered too that when he had (with his eyes closed) reached for what he thought was Um's tail it was really one of the branches of the willow tree! That's what he held clutched so tightly in his trunk right now. For a moment Bo looked around sleepily. What had happened? Where was everybody?

He squinted into the fog. Dimly he saw a big lumpy shape. Was that Um? Slowly he lumbered over to get a better look. No, it was not. It was a rather tall (very tall) box hedge. Bo looked over the hedge into a well-kept garden. Of course Bo did not know it but this was Miss Phoebe's garden. Miss Phoebe was an elderly lady who lived with her elder sister and some chickens. The chickens all had names. She and her sister never ate any of them.

At the moment when Bo's head appeared up on top of the hedge . . . Miss Phoebe with a pan full of chicken feed under her arm was coming out of her back door into her garden. She looked up at Bo's big red head seen dimly through the fog and said . . . "Shoo! Go away from here, horse!"

Bo who was always sensitive to the tone of a voice withdrew his head quickly and went away. He knew when he was not welcome.

Miss Phoebe walked along the garden path to her chicken run grumbling as she went.

"That old horse must be kept tied up. I must speak to

13

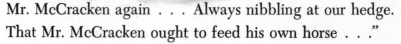

Mr. McCracken again . . . Always nibbling at our hedge. That Mr. McCracken ought to feed his own horse . . ."

Mr. McCracken was the old man who worked the crossbar down at the railroad crossing. He was Miss Phoebe's neighbor across the road. And he had an old sorrel horse who was allowed to wander freely where he would. The neighbors and the children usually gave the old horse carrots and apples and Mr. McCracken did not have to feed his horse very much . . . he was always so full of carrots and apples.

After Miss Phoebe had fed her chickens she went back to her kitchen to prepare breakfast for herself and her sister. Just as she was pouring maple syrup on her flapjacks she suddenly stopped and thought a moment. Then she said out loud:

"He must have been standing on his hind legs!"

"What was that?" asked her sister in amazement, as she cupped her hand around her good ear.

"The old horse!" shouted Miss Phoebe.

14

"What about the old horse?"

"He stuck his head over the top of the hedge . . . nibbling on it again," said Miss Phoebe into her sister's ear. "When I went to feed Antoinette and her brood . . . the old horse stuck his head over the top of the hedge . . ."

"Over the top of the hedge!" exclaimed her sister. "Couldn't have been the old horse. Why that hedge is most ten-foot high . . ."

"It was the old horse," insisted Miss Phoebe as she grasped her knife and fork firmly.

Her sister just closed her eyes, smiled gently and shook her head.

"Tch, tch, tch," she said, when she finally opened her eyes again and stopped shaking her head. "Phoebe, Phoebe, always playful . . . when will you ever grow up?"

Miss Phoebe gasped.

"What has that to do with anything, pray tell?"

"April Fool's Day," said her older sister with a sly, knowing smile. "As if I didn't know this is April Fool's Day . . . Phoebe, Phoebe."

And she closed her eyes again, gently smiled and rocked her head from side to side.

"It was the old horse!" shouted Miss Phoebe, "and he was standing on his hind legs!" And she cut into her pancakes furiously.

15

8:00 A.M. *A Freight Car*

Moves Away

Bo turned away from Miss Phoebe's hedge. Thoughtfully he walked along the road for a while until he found himself on the railroad track. He stood still a moment and turned his head from side to side as he slowly twitched his ropey tail. Then Bo decided to follow the railroad tracks in hopes of finding Um, Jo, Danny and the rest of the circus people.

The railroad track turned around a bend and Bo found himself facing the blank wall of a freight car. He did not step aside. He gently nudged it with his trunk. The freight car moved . . . so Bo absent-mindedly pushed it along

16

as he walked down the track and thought about the best way to find his friends again.

Mr. McCracken was sitting in the snug little house the railroad company provides at railroad crossings for those people who let down the cross-bars and pick them up again. He had let down the cross-bars when the freight train went by and he had lifted them for the circus to march through. That was his regular job.

Suddenly, Mr. McCracken remembered a freight car that had been put aside on a spur of track to clear the way for the long freight train from the west. He reached for his telephone and called the roundhouse.

"Hello, John," he said to the train dispatcher when his connection was completed. "John, I just wanted to remind you to send a switch engine to pick up that freight car that was pushed over to the siding . . . What's that? . . . What's the hurry? . . . That freight car's due at the iron works this morning. It's going to be loaded . . . Sure, I know you know your business . . . But I thought you might forget it . . . Oh, all right, all right . . . So you'll be sending it right along. Good bye, John . . . Now don't get mad . . . So long, John . . ."

Mr. McCracken hung up his telephone receiver and chuckled as he lit his pipe.

"Those young fellers sure get huffy," he said as he settled back in his chair.

And just as he opened his newspaper he heard the rumble of the missing freight car being pushed by Bo along the tracks!

"Some quick service!" said Mr. McCracken shaking his head. "Some quick service! I just telephone and along comes the freight car in a flash! They sure are on their toes up at the roundhouse. Some service!"

Mr. McCracken did not look up as the freight car passed his window and he did not see Bo. But then his eye caught the dateline of his newspaper.

"What's this? . . . April first?" he cried. "April first, eh? Now I wonder . . . Was that an April Fool trick? . . . Sending that freight train along in a flash and so nice and quiet I didn't even hear the engine. That John was playing me for an April Fool! Sure, he must have sent the freight car out before I even called . . . But here's once when I get ahead of him!"

Mr. McCracken grabbed his phone and quickly rang the roundhouse again. And before John at the other end could even say hello Mr. McCracken shouted into the phone.

"And a very, very, very happy April Fool's Day to you, John!" he roared before the astonished John at the other end of the phone could say a word. And then Mr. McCracken slammed his receiver back on the hook.

"There . . . that'll fix him," he laughed. "April Foolin' an old timer like me."

Suddenly Mr. McCracken jumped to his feet and rushed to the levers that control the switches of the railroad tracks. He grabbed one and pulled it quick.

"Phew!" he whistled, "I almost forgot to switch that freight car over to the ironworks tracks."

He thrust his head out of the window of his little house. He could not see the freight car and Bo because of the fog. But he could hear the rumble of the freight car's wheels. Mr. McCracken listened and heard the clackety sound of the wheels as they crossed onto the switched tracks. He sighed with relief.

"In the nick of time," he said. "That April Fool joking John might have caused a wreck with his April foolish tricks . . ." and he grumbled as he settled back with his newspaper again.

9:00 A.M. *Bo Helps the Steam Shovel*

7HE freight car pushed by Bo rolled along until it came
to the end of the spur of track alongside the iron foundry's
loading platform. Since it was rather early in the morning
none of the men who worked in the foundry had come to
work yet. And no one was there to see Bo arrive with the
freight car.

Bo nudged the freight car once or twice after it was
stopped by the cement bumpers at the end of the tracks
and since it would not move he left it there and turned

to amble on again by himself. He heard the sound of people's voices. He flipped one of his ears and shuffled along towards the sound.

A group of people were gathered around the edge of a large excavation. There was a big steam shovel down in the excavation. It looked like a statue of some pre-historic monster. The people stood around waiting for the man who controlled the steam shovel to put on his gloves, climb up on his seat and start the shovel. The steam shovel had been digging up that section of Tannersville for a number of days and all these people always stopped a few minutes to watch the steam shovel bite big mouth-fuls of dirt and gravel out of the big hole every morning before they went to work.

Bo joined them and stood quietly behind the group.

The man finally climbed up to his seat. He pulled a lever here, pushed a lever there, turned a wheel, and then the big steam shovel moved. Slowly the shovel came down, opened its big jagged tooth jaws, dug deep into the earth, and came up again with its jaws clamped shut. It dribbled small rocks and debris as it swivelled and emptied its load on the outer rim of the excavaton. Again and again it bit into the earth and swivelled and deposited its load on the side of the excavation.

The man at the controls was so expert as he handled the

21

levers that the steam shovel moved and acted as if it were a living thing. The people kept their eyes glued to the powerful movement of the big shovel and no one noticed Bo. His little eyes too followed the movement of the big shovel with fascination.

The man driving the steam shovel paid strict attention to his job. He knew the people were watching him and his big shovel, and he was rather proud that they appreciated good steam shovelling. But he did not give them a glance. He just went on with his work. Of course he was used to having people watch his expert steam shov-

elling all day long. And because he knew this early morning audience was his biggest and most important audience he always gave them his best show. During the day
his audience usually consisted of errand boys, a few strag-
glers and some other people either too old or too young
to go to school or go to work.

But these people watching him now he knew were
mainly people who worked in banks and other big business
men who go to work later than other people. The man
on the steam shovel always gave a few extra licks to his
early morning performance.

This morning after depositing one or two smallish steam shovel mouthfuls on the outer rim of the excavation he whirled his shovel around, dipped it fast and with a great powerful thrust drove it into the earth straight at a particularly large boulder. He had planned the day before to move that boulder as his early morning audience watched.

The steam shovel buried its lower jaw deep under the big boulder. The man pulled the lever, snapped the upper jaw down and he pulled the steam shovel up in the air again. But the big boulder was only caught in the front teeth of the steam shovel. It worked loose and flopped back to earth again!

That's the first time anything like that had happened. Everybody's eyes turned to look at the man in the driver's seat. He felt them looking at him and he blushed. Again he attacked the big boulder. Again it was caught only in the front tip of the shovel and back it flopped to earth!

People became restless. They looked at the man driving the steam shovel, then they looked at each other and shrugged their shoulders. Was he losing his touch?

The man was really embarrassed now. He tried again but with no success. Desperately he pulled levers, whirled his shovel and tackled the boulder from the sides . . . to no avail. Beads of perspiration appeared on the man's forehead. Finally in desperation he again attacked the boulder head on. The steam shovel sent up great clouds of smoke and it rocked with effort as it dug under the stubborn boulder. Carefully the man brought the upper jaws down on the boulder.

The boulder teeter-tottered on the front tip of the steam shovel. Everyone held their breath as they waited to see which way the boulder would fall. And just as the boulder started to sway out of the jaws of the steam shovel Bo reached over the heads of the crowds and with his outstretched trunk pushed the undecided boulder safely into the mouth of the steam shovel!

Everyone heaved a great sigh of relief and they turned

their admiring eyes toward the man in the driver's seat. Some people applauded a little and one man said, "Well done!"

Of course everyone had been so intent on watching the battle between the boulder and the steam shovel no one had noticed Bo. And when the battle was at its height there was such a cloud of dust raised and clouds of steam . . . all of it mixed up with the remnant of fog that hung in the air . . . no one could have seen Bo step forward to help the steam shovel even if they had not been paying close attention to that momentous battle.

Bo would have been happy to stay and watch the steam shovel go on with its work if he had not noticed a rather strange look in the eye of the man in the driver's seat.

The man had felt that extra push when Bo lifted the boulder into the jaws of the steam shovel.

"What kind of shenanigans is this?" shouted the man. "Who pushed my steam shovel?"

Then above the cloud of dust and steam the man saw Bo. His mouth fell open.

"What's going on here? . . . Who's bringing on those elephants?" shouted the man when he had recovered from his surprise.

Fortunately, none of the people could hear him above the hiss of the steam and the rattling of the engine that made the steam for the steam shovel. But Bo with his sensitive big ears could hear the man above the noise of the engine and he decided that the man was not really friendly after all. So he turned quietly away and went on looking for his real friends the circus people.

9:10 A.M. *Benny Finds a Parade*

A BOY named Benny Lawrence walked along the street rather slowly. He had been excused from school that morning because he had to go to see the dentist. Instead of running along the street as he usually did, today Benny dragged his feet as he looked for things to happen. He kept hoping he'd meet something or somebody who would postpone his visit to the dentist for just another minute.

Naturally, Benny never expected to meet anything as big and as important as an elephant. But just as he rounded the corner of Stonewall Ave. and Main St. . . . along came Bo, and Benny met him . . . face to face!

28

"A . . . Elephant!" gasped Benny, "A Circus Elephant! . . . Oh boy . . . The parade's coming . . ."

And Benny whirled on his heels and galloped up Main St. like a young Paul Revere shouting to everyone he passed, "The Parade's coming! . . . The Circus Parade's coming!"

Bo lumbered slowly along up Main St. in Benny's wake.

At that hour of the morning with the children in school, the men at work and most of the ladies busy with housework there were not many people walking along Main St. Some storekeepers getting their stores ready for the day looked up at Bo as he passed and went back to work.

When Benny breathlessly arrived at the busiest intersection of Tannersville . . . where Main St. crosses State . . . he shouted to the policeman directing traffic in the center of the street:

"Hey! . . . Parade's coming! . . . The Circus Parade's coming!"

And Benny picked the best spot in the world to watch a circus parade . . . the corner of State and Main Street . . . and he dug his heels into the curb and stood there and waited for the parade to come along.

The traffic policeman looked at his wrist watch and angrily muttered to himself.

"Say . . . It's only half-past nine! They should have told me about the change. They ought to change their permit. That parade's not due till twelve o'clock. Gotta good mind to stop them altogether . . . Oh, well . . ."

The traffic policeman blew his whistle and stopped all traffic going across Main St. and he waved at all automobiles and trucks that were travelling along Main St. to pull over to the curb. Then he stood along the side of the street and waited for the parade to come along.

Some people came out of their stores and stood alongside of Benny firmly rooted to the curb. They too waited. After a while down the middle of Main Street came Bo.

"Here it is!" shouted the policeman. "Stand back, everybody! . . . Give them room!"

Along came Bo. Benny, the policeman and the others watched him come. They watched him pass. And they looked after him when he had gone by. For a few minutes after Bo was gone the policeman waited for more paraders. But no one came along. He looked up and down the street. Then he scratched his head.

"Looks like a pretty thin parade this year," he said to no one in particular. Then he blew his whistle three sharp blasts and started traffic going again.

"Some parade!" said Benny out loud. "Some parade . . . Betcha it's not gonna be much of a circus either . . . Some parade . . . Huh . . . Just one old Red, White and Blue Elephant . . ."

And Benny went on to the dentist.

9:30 A.M. *Mr. Mason*

Has a Headache

Mr. Mason, the principal of Benny's school, came down to breakfast wearing a worried look.

"My dear," he said to his wife as he finished his breakfast, "I believe this is going to be a very trying day."

"A trying day, Mr. Mason?" said his wife (she always called her husband Mr. Mason).

"Yes," said Mr. Mason, "somehow I feel this is going to be a very trying day. Better pack my headache pills in my brief case. I'm sure I'm going to need them before the day is over. Now what is my schedule?"

Mr. Mason flipped open a little black book in which he marked off the schedule of his day's activities.

"Oh, yes . . . m-m . . . yes, April First, morning assembly . . . then lunch with the Parent-Teachers committee . . . m-m, then . . . Oh, there it is. A half-holiday for the circus! M-m . . . April First, All Fool's Day and the circus both on the same day . . . Dear me, dear me, I feel my headache coming on."

Mr. Mason wore that worried look on his face all the way to school. And after the children had marched into the school assembly to the tune of "The March of the Wooden Soldiers" and after they had all pledged allegiance to the flag of the United States of America and sung the school song "The Garnet and Grey Forever" . . . Mr. Mason made a short speech as he did every assembly morning. He began as he usually did.

"Good morning, girls and boys."

And the girls and boys in one great chorus responded.

"Good-morn-ing-Mr. Ma-son."

This morning Mr. Mason forgot to say as he usually did, "I am happy to see so many bright and smiling faces," but got right down to the meat of his speech.

"Boys and girls," he said, "who can tell me why today, the first of April, is a special day?"

A sea of hands shot up all over the Assembly room.

"That girl there . . . you with the red ribbons, speak up loud," said Mr. Mason, picking an eager little girl in the third row.

"Because it's Friday," said the little girl, shyly.

"H-m-m . . . yes," said Mr. Mason. "Does anyone else have any other reason why April 1st is a special day?"

"Because the circus came to town this morning," said one big boy with a grin when he was chosen.

"Because it's April Fool's Day," said another boy quickly. A wave of delighted giggles swept the assembly room. Some people clapped their hands together and two boys shouted, "Hooray."

Mr. Mason with his lips set in a tight smile raised his hands for silence.

"Yes, that's right. That's the answer I wanted. It is April Fool's Day or All Fools' Day and the circus is here . . ."

Then Mr. Mason explained how April Fool's Day or the celebration of All Fools' Day may have come about. That it was a celebration of the Spring "Vernal Equinox." Mr. Mason could see by the expression on the children's faces that the Vernal Equinox meant nothing at all to them. So he explained what that meant.

"It means," he said, "the time when the sun crosses the celestial Equator towards the north . . . that is called the Spring Vernal Equinox . . ."

The children's faces still looked blank.

"Well," said Mr. Mason briskly, "it has something to do with the coming of spring."

"Now, April Fool's Day is celebrated all over the world. In India it is called the Feast of Huli . . . In Scotland it is called 'hunting the gowk' . . . Gowk is Scottish for cuckoo . . . In France a person who is fooled on this day is called 'Poisson d'Avril' . . . That's French and it means April fish . . ."

By this·time the children were getting a little restless and Mr. Mason hurried on with his explanation of the beginning and meaning of·April Fool's Day.

"Now, April fish really means a foolish young fish that can easily be caught . . . Now then, we all know what April Fool's Day or All Fools' Day means and we know it is celebrated all over the world . . . Isn't that so?"

All the children nodded their heads and in one voice they said, "Yes, Mr. Mason."

"But," continued Mr. Mason, "we are not going to cele-brate April Fool's Day here in school or around the school grounds. We are going to study our lessons, aren't we?"

There were scattered nods through the Assembly room and the chorus of "Yes, Mr. Mason" was very weak.

"And no one will even think about April Fool's Day this morning . . ."

Suddenly Mr. Mason stopped talking. His eyes lit up with a wonderful idea.

"Let's not even call this day April Fool's Day at all . . . Let's all call it the Vernal Equinox . . . now everyone repeat after me. Vernal Equinox."

And everyone including the teachers chanted.

"Ver-nal-Equi-nox."

"That's it. Vernal Equinox . . . Now then, if we do our work and there are no April Fool pranks . . . I mean Vernal Equinox pranks . . . we shall have a half-holiday and all of us who want to may go to see the circus this afternoon . . ."

The children were delighted. Mr. Mason beamed at their

37

happy faces for a moment. Then he raised his hands for silence again.

"Remember now, no Vernal Equinox pranks," he said, seriously. "And now I want to say a word or two to the boys who are on our baseball team which will have its first session of spring practice this morning . . ."

Silence reigned in the Assembly room. You could have heard a pin drop if anyone had wanted to drop a pin.

"Boys," said Mr. Mason, very serious now. "Boys . . . remember Courage and Fortitude . . . That's what counts both on the playfield and in life."

Then Mr. Mason nodded to a teacher who sat at the piano. She struck two chords. All the children stood up and again to the music of the "Wooden Soldiers" the children two by two marched out of the Assembly room.

Mr. Mason wiped his forehead with a snowy white handkerchief. And when the last two children had gone out the door he said to the piano-playing teacher . . .

"I've got a headache."

10:00 A.M. *A Baseball Becomes Invisible*

$\mathcal{N}$OTHING remarkable happened during the first half of the morning at Mr. Mason's school. But about mid-morning Bo, the lost elephant, in his coat of red, white and blue paint wandered down the quiet street past the school and things began to stir.

The upper grade boys under the watchful eye of the teacher in charge of physical education were out in the boys' yard practicing baseball. There was a high wooden fence around the yard and none of the boys saw Bo, nor did he see them. But he heard them and he stopped to listen to their cheerful voices.

After a series of setting-up exercises the boys practiced hitting the ball. The schoolyard was full of fielders. Every boy except the one whose turn it was at bat and the pitcher and the catcher was a fielder. But they did not have much to do since the boy who pitched was a very good pitcher and almost no one hit the ball.

One boy after another gripped the bat, swung furiously once, twice, and a third time and they were out. Until along came one big eighth-grade boy (nicknamed Babe Ruth) who everyone knew was a famous slugger. This big boy stood quietly and calmly waiting for the pitch. Everybody shouted, "Attaboy, Babe" or "Hit a home run, Babe . . . Knock it over the fence . . . Attaboy, Babe."

Babe stood at home plate swinging his bat menacingly waiting for the first pitch. The pitcher wound up, along came the ball . . . and crack . . . Babe swung and he did hit the ball right over the fence!

Everyone turned and watched the ball sail over the fence and before their admiring eyes could turn back to the field again the ball came sailing back and landed at the feet of Babe!

"What happened?" everyone wanted to know. "It went over!" shouted some. "It didn't . . . it didn't," shouted others. "It bounced off the top . . . It didn't go over the fence. It bounced off the top of the fence!"

40

The teacher in charge of physical education blew her whistle furiously.

"Quiet, everybody, quiet," she cried. "Now let's try that again. Pitch that ball once more. We won't count the last one."

Again the pitcher got set to pitch and again Babe waited at the plate with his bat. And again Bo who stood on the other side of the fence waited. Because it was Bo who had caught the ball in the tip of his trunk when it came over the fence and he had promptly thrown it back.

That was one of the tricks Bo learned in the circus. Jo,

Um and Bo were trained to act like baseball players. That part of their performance always delighted the audience.

The pitcher tightened his belt, pulled the peak of his cap, secretively wrapped his finger around the ball as he squinted down the field at the waiting batter. Babe wagged his bat back and forth slowly like the twitching tail of a tiger waiting to spring. It was a tense moment.

Suddenly the pitcher whipped his arm out and threw his very best pitch . . . a sort of speedy, fadeaway, razzle-dazzle curve . . .

Babe swung and caught the ball on the tip of his bat. Up it sailed . . . up . . . up . . . and over the fence again. There was no doubt about it this time. The ball did go over the fence! But there were no cheers because just as promptly the ball came sailing back again!

Once more the ball was returned to the home plate. This time the catcher was ready for it and he caught the ball.

For a moment no one said anything. Then the teacher in charge of physical education walked over to the place where the ball had gone over the fence. She wrapped sharply on one of the boards of the fence with her knuckles, then she called out.

"Thank you, whoever you are, for returning our ball. But please don't do it again. We have a lot of very anxious, very eager fielders in here and we really are quite capable of getting our own ball . . . Now please go away."

Her voice though loud sounded quite friendly to Bo on the other side, so he stayed right where he was and waited for more balls to be tossed over the fence.

"Now, then," said the teacher, "that takes care of that . . . Next boy at bat."

No one knows whether the next boy at bat was a good hitter or whether he had been inspired by Babe. But he closed his eyes tight and swung hard at the first pitch and sent a hot grounder down past second base.

After a bit of a scramble among the many fielders in back of second base the ball was finally retrieved by one boy. He threw the ball hard and fast to first base but he threw wild and high. Once more the ball popped over the fence . . . and once more Bo caught it and tossed it back. This time the ball landed just in back of second base.

The teacher in charge of physical education frowned.

"Let me have that ball," she said in a quiet tense voice. "We'll put a stop to this."

One of the boys ran over with the ball. The teacher took it and walked stiffly to the fence. She stood there quietly a moment, then she tossed the ball (under-handed) over the fence. Bo on the other side caught it and threw it back. Once more the teacher threw the ball over and again Bo just as promptly threw it back.

43

"That will do!" said the teacher in a loud voice. Then she rapped on the fence with her knuckles and she said angrily, "Now then, I shall toss the ball over the fence for the last time. You . . . whoever you are, let it lie where it lands. This ball is school property . . . and if you touch it again I shall report you to the proper authorities."

The teacher waited a moment, then very deliberately, she threw the ball over the fence for the last time. She

waited one minute, two minutes, three minutes. Bo on the other side who had sensed the anger in her voice had become rather weary of tossing the ball . . . And, too, he heard from one of the open classroom windows some interesting sounds. Bo decided to investigate the source of the sound and quietly walked around the side of the school building.

The teacher waited a full four minutes by her wrist watch.

"There now," she said triumphantly. "That did it. Now I'll get the ball myself. You boys gather up the bats and gloves. Baseball practice is over."

She walked to the gate of the boys' yard, swung the door open and looked down the street. Then she looked up the street. There was no sign of a living soul! And there was no sign of the ball!

"Where are you . . . Whoever you are?" she called out.

Of course no one answered since there was no one either coming or going along the empty street. The teacher looked behind the gate door . . . and up and down the street again.

"Well . . . where are you?" she repeated as she raised her voice. "Listen to me, whoever you are . . . You'd better bring that baseball right back . . ."

She waited in silence for a moment.

45

"See here," she said in a real loud voice now, "if this is your idea of an April Fool joke you'd better stop it immediately! You're fooling around with school property! . . . If you don't return that baseball at once . . . whoever you are . . . I'll report you to Mr. Mason!"

The teacher in charge of physical education waited for "whoever it was" to answer. Then she slammed the gate of the Boys' Yard shut!

10:30 A.M. *Bo Visits*

the Second Grade

$\mathcal{W}$ITH the missing baseball curled up in his trunk Bo quietly walked around to the side of the school building. As he passed a window with a flower pot on its ledge he lifted his trunk and placed the ball alongside the flower pot. Then absent-mindedly his trunk wrapped itself around the flower pot. He carried the flower pot along with him until he found the open classroom window from which the interesting sound came.

It was one of the second grade windows. The children were having their regular singing lesson. Bo stood beneath the window, his head cocked to one side and one big ear spread, as he listened to their singing. His trunk swayed from side to side in time to the music. He liked good music. The circus band always played good and loud and so did the calliope as it blasted away at the end of the circus parade. So he enjoyed the good loud singing of the children of the second grade.

The children finished one song, then after a short silence, led by their teacher they started another. Up went Bo's both ears. His eyes lit up with surprise. Bo knew that song! It was "Three Cheers for the Red, White and Blue," the song to which Jo, Um and Bo always began their Grand Finale act! That was the song to which they marched into the big arena walking on their blue hind legs and waving the small American flags in their lifted red trunks.

Bo swayed from side to side. And just as the second grade children were about to shout out the last line "Three Cheers for the Red, White and Blue" Bo stood up on his hind legs and waved the flower pot he had picked up from the window in his upheld trunk. His head appeared in the second grade window. The children stopped singing at once. Some of them squealed.

"Look! . . . Pink Elephants! . . . Pink Elephants and flower pots!"

When the singing stopped Bo let himself sink back on

all four legs again. The second grade teacher had not seen
him when his head appeared at the window. She was standing at the front of the class, her back to the window as she
tapped out the words of the song that were written on the
blackboard. At the cry of "Pink Elephants" she whirled
around too late to see Bo.

The teacher tapped her desk sharply with her pointer.

49

"Attention . . . What's going on?" she demanded.

Some children made vague gestures toward the window. One little girl swallowed the lump in her throat and repeated in a very low voice what many of them had squealed out loud just a moment before, "Pink Elephants . . . and flower pots."

"Nonsense. There are no such things as Pink Elephants," said the second grade teacher sternly. But she did not deny there were flower pots. "Children, remember what Mr. Mason said, if there is no April Fooling . . . er . . . Vernal Equinoxing we may all go to see the circus parade . . . But right now let's not even think of circuses . . . Eyes front everyone!"

The class with some difficulty stopped looking towards the window.

"Here," said the teacher, "I've written the words for our next song, 'When Johnny Comes Marching Home.' It's not hard. Now let's begin. I'll sing it first . . ."

The second grade teacher always began to teach her class the songs they were to sing on some holiday or festival months in advance. Today on the first of April they were learning to sing their Decoration Day songs.

The teacher blew her pitch-pipe, then she sang "When Johnny Comes Marching Home" as she pointed to the words on the blackboard.

"Very well, class," she said, when she had finished. "Now let's all try to sing together . . . One . . . two . . . One . . . two. Begin . . ." and the teacher blew her pitch-pipe again.

The class began slowly but they gathered momentum. Before the teacher's pointer had reached the third line of the song they were singing along almost all of them together and naturally good and loud.

Bo's ears perked up. He recognized that song too! Slowly he began to sway from side to side. He placed the flower pot on the window ledge of the second grade class and then with a deep sigh and a grunt his head came down, his hind quarters went up and he stood on his front legs. Just the way he always did with Jo and Um when the circus bands played that song.

The children went on singing. They tried to keep their eyes fixed to the front of the room but now and then their eyes would turn to the window. When Bo's blue-painted hind legs, ropey tail and hind quarters appeared at the window their singing weakened, slowed down and finally stopped altogether.

"Well now . . . Now what's the matter!" demanded their teacher impatiently.

"Blue Elephants!" said the class in one awe-stricken voice.

51

"Blue Elephants!" repeated the teacher, "BLUE ELE-
PHANTS! Why, of all the . . . Blue Elephants! Where
are the Blue Elephants?"

The whole class pointed to the window.

Of course when the singing had stopped Bo had brought
his hind legs down. He was only trained to stand on his
front legs as long as he heard the music of "When Johnny
Comes Marching Home" and when the teacher looked at
the window there was no sign of him.

"I can't see any Blue Elephants," said the teacher. Then
she saw the flower pot on the window ledge. "Who put this
strange flower pot on our window sill?"

The teacher picked up the flower pot and for a moment
the class was silent. Then a little boy raised his hand
timidly.

"Did you put this flower pot on our window sill?" asked the teacher. "Is this your flower pot?"

"No, ma'am," said the boy. "Maybe it belongs to the pink elephants."

The teacher thought a moment as she looked at the children. Then she gestured to the class monitor.

"I'm going to the principal's office. Monitor, take charge of the class."

The second grade teacher found Mr. Mason nervously pacing the floor with a baseball gripped in one hand when she bustled into his office.

"Now what?" said Mr. Mason.

"Mr. Mason . . . my children are so wrought up that they're seeing elephants . . . pink ones. Just as we were singing . . ." began the second grade teacher.

Mr. Mason interrupted her.

"Where did you get my flower pot?" he asked.

"Your flower pot!" said the bewildered teacher. "Is it your flower pot? . . . My children said it belonged to the pink elephants . . ."

"Pink elephants!" exclaimed Mr. Mason. "What is this about pink elephants?"

"And blue elephants!" added the teacher.

"Blue elephants? . . . Pink elephants?" cried Mr. Mason. "Will you please tell me what is going on. I find my flower pot missing and in its place I found this baseball . . . what have pink and blue elephants got to do with my flower pot? . . . And now this baseball! . . ."

At that moment the teacher in charge of physical education came rushing into the office. Her arms were full of baseball bats and gloves.

"Mr. Mason," she began, breathlessly, "our baseball disappeared in the strangest way . . . I'm very much afraid that someone deliberately took our baseball . . ."

Then when she saw the baseball in Mr. Mason's hands she interrupted herself.

"Oh . . . Mr. Mason, is that our baseball?"

Mr. Mason with a bewildered look on his face slowly sat down on his desk.

"Ladies, let's be calm. Let's begin from the beginning. This is getting rather confusing. Now please, tell your story," he said to the second grade teacher.

As quickly and as simply as she could, the second grade teacher told what she believed happened in her classroom. Then the teacher in charge of physical education told what she believed happened in the boys' yard.

When they both were done Mr. Mason sat a moment deep in thought. Then he arose from his desk and marched up and down his office . . . twice. Then he stood still and

54

looked at the clock hanging on his office wall and he checked it with his wrist watch.

"Hm-m, ladies," he said, "there's no question in my mind some very strange things are happening in this school today. Your reports on pink and blue elephants, flying flower pots, disappearing and reappearing baseballs convince me that whatever is happening is bigger than all of us. Let's not fight it. I believe the children are so excited with thoughts about the circus and probably with the Vernal Equinox . . . we may as well surrender."

A weak smile spread over Mr. Mason's face. The teachers looked at each other and said nothing, waiting for Mr. Mason to continue.

"Ladies, my clock and watch say it is now 10:33. Is that one thing we can all believe that is correct?"

Both teachers looked at their wrist watches, then together they nodded their heads.

"Very well then," concluded Mr. Mason, "in exactly five minutes, at 10:38, I shall ring the dismissal bell. Our half-holiday will begin and we all can go home and get ready to go to the circus."

And Mr. Mason placed the baseball in the hands of the physical education teacher and the second grade teacher gave the flower pot to Mr. Mason and they all smiled. Then they went about their business.

Mr. Carlin Gets a Clue

D<small>ANNY</small> M<small>ORGAN</small> and Mr. Carlin came rattling along the Main St. of Tannersville in a small truck. They stopped at the office of Tannersville's only newspaper . . . the Tannersville Clarion, and they rushed through the door.

"Where's the city editor?" demanded Mr. Carlin of a man wearing a green eye shade who sat behind the desk.

"I'm the city editor," said the man. "And I'm the night editor, managing editor, advertising manager, reporter, copy reader . . . I'm the works. I'm the whole Tannersville Clarion. What can I do for you, Mister?"

"Mr. Tannersville Clarion, I've come to do something for you . . . Stop the presses! Tear out the front page!"

cried Mr. Carlin, his voice rising in excitement. "I'm gonna give you the biggest, the most important story that the Tannersville Clarion ever printed . . ."

"Just a minute, mister, you don't have to shout. I'm not deaf," said the man with the green eye shade. "My name's Clifton B. Lawrence. You're a stranger in town or you'd know that. I haven't seen you around and I know everybody."

"My name's Carlin," said Mr. Carlin. "I'm the Carlin of the Barton and Carlin Circus . . . The B. & C. Circus. The C. stands for Carlin. That's me. This is Danny Morgan. He works for us."

"Oh, you're circus people," said Mr. Lawrence. He wearily picked up a pencil and pad. "All right, get on with it. My press starts rolling in just half an hour . . ."

"Mister, here's the big story." Mr. Carlin rested both his hands on Mr. Lawrence's desk and leaned towards him. "We . . . just . . . lost . . . A Red, White and Blue . . . Elephant!"

"What's that you said? You just lost a Red, White and Blue *Elephant!*"

"Yes sir," said Mr. Carlin, dramatically. Then he went on quickly, "We just lost a Red, White and Blue Elephant. His name is Bo . . . spelt . . . B . . . O . . . ! Now this elephant Bo is one of the top stars of one of the most colossal finale acts the B. & C. Circus ever put on. Bo is about ten feet tall, weighs about five ton, has light brown eyes . . . and he's painted up red, white and blue. Now it seems somewhere along the route about six o'clock this morning he disappeared into the misty dawn . . . Just vanished into thin air . . . It was just as the B. & C. Circus started to . . ."

Mr. Lawrence pushed back his green eye shade and stopped writing. He threw his pencil down in disgust, then he looked up at Mr. Carlin.

"Hog-wash!" he said.

"What say?" asked Mr. Carlin in surprise.

"I said . . . Hog-wash!" repeated Mr. Lawrence louder. "Yes sir, it sounds like hog-wash to me. A red, white and blue elephant disappearing into the misty dawn! . . . Mister, I'm running a family newspaper that prints the truth and nothing but the truth . . . What you're telling me is hog-wash! That's what I call it. Go away, mister, I'm a busy man. I've got a newspaper to get out."

"But . . . But . . . But," Mr. Carlin sputtered.

"Look here, Mister Circus Man," said Mr. Lawrence,

pointing with his pencil across the desk at Mr. Carlin's nose. "I have written a story about your circus opening up in Tannersville today. It's a good front-page story. And I put in it all the blabber-dash you sent me about your big show. And I set up the type for the advertising you paid for . . . It's not much. But if you want to get more space in the Tannersville Clarion you'll have to pay for it same as anyone else . . . Yes sir, you'll pay the same as the butcher, the baker or the candlestick maker . . . or the undertaker or anyone else that's got something to sell."

For a moment Mr. Carlin was speechless. Danny Morgan stepped forward and spoke up hesitatingly.

"What Mr. Carlin's been saying is the honest truth, Mister. I was a-walking along with Jo, the first elephant . . ."

"Who are you?" said Mr. Lawrence.

"He's Danny Morgan, my assistant elephant man," said Mr. Carlin. Then he placed his hand on Danny's shoulder. "Just a minute, Danny . . ."

Mr. Carlin stood in silence for a moment as he looked with sincere, sober eyes straight into the eyes of the man across the desk.

"Mr. Tannersville Clarion . . . er . . . Mr. Lawrence I mean . . . I want to tell you something," he said with a deep sad tremble in his voice. "Mr. Lawrence . . . I love elephants! . . . Yes sir, I love elephants. I've been an

59

elephant man all my life, man and boy. Do you think for one minute feeling the way I do about elephants I'd come in here with a trumped up story about a lost red, white and blue elephant . . . if it weren't the truth, the whole truth and nothing but the truth?"

Mr. Lawrence squirmed uncomfortably in his chair. His eyes fell and he looked down at his desk. Then he looked up again.

"Lookit here, mister. I'm running a newspaper. When someone comes in here and tells me a story about a red, white and blue elephant disappearing into thin air on this day," and the man drew a heavy black line under the date, 'April 1st' on his desk calendar. He paused a moment and gave Mr. Carlin a long look before he went on.

"Yessir, when somebody comes in here on April 1st I figure . . . Say, do you know how many times I've answered my telephone this morning to tell people this is not the fish market? I guess I must have told another dozen smart alecks that called up that I am not Mr. Pinhead and I won't please call Mrs. Pinhead to the phone . . . I've had enough April Fool jokes so far this morning . . ."

"But this is not an April Fool joke," said Danny Morgan sincerely. "Honest, mister, that elephant Bo disappeared somewhere along the road to the big meadow."

And quickly before Mr. Lawrence or Mr. Carlin could

stop him Danny told as much as he knew about the mysterious disappearance of the red, white and blue elephant named Bo.

Mr. Lawrence was impressed with the sincerity of Danny's story but after thinking a moment he shook his head impatiently.

"See here, I'm busy. I've gotta get back to work. Here's my last word. I am not running any story on a disappearing elephant . . ." Then he interrupted himself. "Say . . . wait a minute. I just thought of something. Maybe there's a real story angle in this after all . . ."

Mr. Carlin and Danny held their breath as they waited for Mr. Lawrence to speak again.

"Here's the angle. Is this elephant dangerous? Will he do any damage to private property? . . . Or kill somebody? . . . Or something like that? Now *that* would be a news story!"

"Dangerous! Damage property! Kill somebody!" Mr. Carlin and Danny repeated in one horror-stricken voice.

"Why, mister, that elephant is as gentle as a kitten," said Mr. Carlin emphatically. "He wouldn't hurt a fly. Why, sir, he don't even switch his tail and chase the flies off his hide for fear of bruising them. That elephant Bo is the kindest . . . the gentlest . . . the most considerate . . ."

Mr. Lawrence shook his head slowly from side to side.

"Well, that does it," he said. "So there's no story . . ." and Mr. Lawrence went back to work.

Mr. Carlin looked at Danny, shrugged his shoulders and they both started for the door. Before they got to it the door was opened from the outside. Benny Lawrence stuck his head into the open doorway.

"Hey, Pop, can I go to the circus?" he began talking before he got into the room.

"Benny!" said Mr. Lawrence sharply. "What's up? What are you doing out of school this time of the morning?"

"Had to go to the dentist, Pop. Remember?" said Benny. "Remember this filling fell out last night."

Benny opened his mouth as wide as he could and pointed to one of his back molars.

"All right . . . so you got it filled again. Now shut your mouth and tell me why you've not gone back to school yet," said his father.

"I did go back, but we were excused for the circus. Can I go, Pop? Huh? Can I, Pop? But I bet it's not gonna be much of a circus. Saw the parade before I went to the dentist . . . But can I go anyway, Pop?"

"What's that you said?" asked Mr. Carlin as he quickly pulled out his big gold watch. "You saw the parade? You couldn't have seen the parade. It's only 11 o'clock . . ."

"Did too see the parade," insisted Benny. "Saw it at the

corner of State and Main St. Some parade . . . Huh! . . .
Just one old red, white and blue elephant . . ."

"One . . . Red . . . White . . . and Blue Elephant!" repeated Mr. Carlin, Danny and Mr. Lawrence in one hoarse
whisper as they stared at Benny.

"Yeah . . . one red, white and blue elephant . . .
What's the matter? I didn't do anything. I was just going
to the dentist . . . And along came the circus parade . . .
just one old painted up elephant."

Mr. Carlin grabbed Benny firmly by the shoulders.

"Think, boy! Think back carefully," he said in a tense
voice. "You saw this elephant. Where? Exactly WHERE?"

"Like I said," said Benny squirming out of Mr. Carlin's
grasp. "I saw him at the corner of State and Main."

"Yes . . . Yes . . . go on," said Mr. Carlin. "Can you
remember exactly what time that was?"

"Let's see," said Benny, "just after I got excused from
school . . . and I walked sort of slow . . . then I ran
sort of quick . . . I don't know."

"And then what happened? Which way did he go?"

"Guess he just went on up Main St.," said Benny. "I
hadda go to the dentist over on State St. . . . Yeah, he
just went up Main."

"Was he going fast or slow?"

Benny thought a moment.

"Well, sort of slow, I guess. Yeah, sort of slow."

"Fine! Fine!" said Mr. Carlin, all smiles now. "That gives us a clue. We ought to pick him up pretty quick now . . ."

Mr. Carlin quickly looked at his watch again.

"Say, it's just 11 o'clock! I gotta start our parade at noon . . . You've got a bright lad here," he said to Mr. Lawrence, and to Benny he said, "Son, you just wait till you see the real circus parade. It's the Biggest, the most Colossal, the most Stupendous . . . And don't you worry about the B. & C. Circus not being much of a circus. It's the Biggest, the most Colossal, the most Stupendous . . . Here you are. Here's a handful of tickets. Bring your friends and see for yourself."

Mr. Carlin pushed a fistful of tickets into the eager hands of Benny and ran out the door followed by Danny. Just before Danny went out the door he turned and with a big glowing smile he said, "Thanks, kid!"

Mr. Lawrence rushed out from behind his desk.

"I'll put a couple of lines in the Lost and Found column," he shouted after Mr. Carlin and Danny. "Just two lines: 'Lost one Red, White and Blue Elephant. Please return to the B. & C. Circus.' O.K.?"

"O.K.," shouted Mr. Carlin and he raced his truck away.

12:00 NOON *The Cows*

Meet a Stranger

THE Colossal, Stupendous B. & C. Circus parade marched at high noon up the Main Street of Tannersville without one of the circus' brightest performing stars because at that hour that bright star Bo was drinking water from a brook in a pasture alongside of two black and white cows.

He had wandered away from Mr. Mason's school, crossed a few empty lots and walked out into the open fields. He remembered that circus people always set up their big tents in broad open fields. So that's where he went to look for them.

The cows that drank alongside of him were a little surprised when he first showed up in the pasture but since he was gentle as Mr. Carlin said he was, they were not at all disturbed by his presence. But the farmer who owned the cows was!

He was slowly driving his horse and wagon on the road that skirted his cow pasture when he happened to look up and see Bo standing there at the brook with the cows. He stopped his horse short, pulled out his handkerchief, cleaned his glasses and looked again.

"Hey, there!" he shouted. "Get out of my pasture."

Bo lifted his head, looked at the farmer, and didn't move a step. He slowly lifted his dripping trunk and waved it high in the air. That must have scared the farmer because he slapped the reins on his old horse's back and raced him up the hill to his house.

The moment he brought his wagon to a rattling stop he jumped to the ground and dashed into the kitchen.

"There's a wild elephant down in the pasture," he shouted to his wife. "His head's all red . . . covered with blood! He's down there with the cows . . . Gotta phone for help . . ."

His wife, who had just taken a cake out of the oven and was whipping up a chocolate frosting for her cake, did not even turn away from her work.

"I've been waiting all morning," she said calmly, "wait-ing until you'd remember that this was the day . . . All right then, April Fool . . ."

"I'm not April Fooling!" shouted the farmer.

"All right, then you're not April Fooling," said his wife, still calm. "But stop stomping around my kitchen . . . You'll make my cake fall. Just took it out of the oven."

"But I'm telling you I saw an elephant! A big red-headed elephant down in the cow pasture!"

You needn't shout . . . You're getting pretty red-headed yourself shouting that way," said his wife.

"I'm not shouting!" shouted the farmer. "Come and look for yourself . . . I'm telling you I saw a big . . ."

"I know . . . I know," said his wife. "I know you saw a big red-headed elephant killing the cows down in the pasture."

"Not killing the cows . . . Drinking from the brook with the cows."

"Oh, drinking with the cows," said his wife with a patient smile. "Well, I've got a minute while my cake cools . . . If you must have your fun . . . Was it last year or the year before when you came along with the story that Betsy's pretty little new calf had climbed up on the barn roof? Yes, it was April First last year . . . My, the way I ran for the ladder . . . And the way you hollered April

67

Fool! Dear me, all right, let's get on to the pasture if you must have your fun . . ."

The farmer said not a word. He got his shotgun and he grimly kept his mouth clamped shut as he drove his horse as fast as he would go down the hill to the cow pasture.

"Well . . . Where's your wild and wooly red-headed elephant?" asked his wife when they reached the pasture.

The two cows sat quietly chewing their cud. Bo was gone!

"He was there, I'm telling you," insisted the farmer. "Right there by the brook. A big wild one . . . Almost as high as a . . ."

"Seems to me if there had been a wild beast in that field those cows wouldn't be peacefully sitting around minding their own business. Now you've had your fun. Say it."

"Say what?" asked the farmer.

"Say April Fool, of course," said his wife. "I'm a bigger April Fool than you think, for letting you catch me year after year. All right, take me back to the house. I've got to spread the frosting on my cake before it gets hard in the bowl."

2:00 P.M. *Bo Finds the Circus*

$\mathcal{M}$R. CARLIN and Danny had raced up and down the streets of Tannersville as long as they dared before the parade was due to start.

"Danny," said Mr. Carlin finally. "We can't take any more time looking for Bo. We've got to get back and start the parade. The show must go on. We'll have to parade without him . . ."

"But, Mr. Carlin, can't we . . ." Danny began.

"No, Danny . . . We can't do anything. Our duty is to our public. The show must go on," said Mr. Carlin, sadly. "Don't worry though. We'll look for him right after today's show. We're bound to find him before tonight's perform-ance."

The B. & C. Circus parade was pretty well received by the people who stood along the curbs. It was as Mr. Carlin promised both colossal and stupendous but it seemed to many to lack something. That was because all the clowns, the men in the bands, the beautiful be-spangled ladies and gentlemen (who were acrobats in the show and rode horses in the parade) and the cowboys and Indians . . . all knew Bo was lost and they all worried about him.

Even the animal paraders seemed to be a little low in spirits. The horses didn't prance. The lion in his gilded wagon cage did not roar even once during the whole length of the march. The tiger didn't prowl back and forth in his cage as he usually did. He just sulked on his cage floor. The camels' humps wilted sadly to one side. And ending up the parade the steam calliope which had struck a leak in one of its pipes wheezed sadly when the man who played it hit that note.

"We didn't make much of a showing," said Mr. Barton to Mr. Carlin later as they both leaned against the gilded wagon from which the tickets were sold. "Guess we won't have much of a ticket sale this afternoon."

Mr. Carlin who was chewing a straw did not say anything. He was just trying to figure out where he'd go to look for Bo right after the afternoon's performance was over. Mr. Barton anxiously watched the thin lines of people who gathered at the ticket window for a few minutes.

"There's something funny going on, Carlin," he said after a while. "The crowd isn't showing up. We'll not half fill our tent by the time the first act begins."

Mr. Carlin took the straw out of his mouth and stopped thinking about Bo.

"Say there, you're right, Barton," he said. "It sure seems quiet around here . . . What this show needs is better barkers . . . I'll show those barkers how to bark . . . You can't hardly hear them."

Mr. Carlin climbed up on a big box and began to shout.

"Hur-ray! . . . Hur-ray! . . . Hur-ray! . . . Get your tickets for the big Show! The most Colossal . . . The most Stupendous . . . The most Dazzling Spectacle of the Ages . . . Hur-ray! . . . Hur-ray! . . . Hur-ray! . . . Get your tickets for the big show . . . See the death-defying daredevils . . . See the most hilarious, side-splitting clowns

in the world! . . . See the most brilliant, the most fasci-
nating . . . the most glorious animal act in the world . . .
See the most . . ."

Mr. Carlin thought of the missing Bo again as he shouted
about "the most glorious animal act in the world" . . . and
he stopped barking. Slowly he climbed down from the box.

"Can't do it, Barton," he said sadly. "Can't bark good
when I think of that lost elephant."

For another few minutes they leaned against the gilded
ticket wagon in silence. Mr. Carlin went back to chewing
a straw. Suddenly he pulled it out of his mouth.

"Lookit here, Barton," he said. "Did you notice there's
no girls and boys in those lines. All of them are grown
up people! What's happened to the kids in this town?—
What's keeping them away from this circus? It's the
strangest sight I ever saw. A circus with no boys and
girls around . . . What's up?"

Mr. Carlin and Mr. Barton looked around at the thin crowd.

"It sure looks mighty queer, Carlin," said Mr. Barton. "Are you sure there's no county fair . . . or special events going on over in town . . ."

"No special events would keep a good red-blooded boy or girl away from a circus," said Mr. Carlin. "No sir, there's something happening . . . Something's going on. Maybe we should not have opened on April Fools' Day . . . Maybe the boys and girls are April Fooling the whole Circus by staying away . . ."

Mr. Barton and Mr. Carlin waited as long as they could before they started their circus. It always started at 2:30 in the afternoon. They waited until 2:30 . . . then they

waited almost until 2:40 before they started the Big Show.

"It's no use, Barton," said Mr. Carlin. "The audience is getting impatient. We've got to start the show even though our tent's only half-full and none of the children came."

"Guess you're right," said Mr. Barton. "I'll go round and give the signal to begin."

The Barton and Carlin Circus started like all good circuses start with a Grand Parade by all of the performers around the arena. Mr. Barton started to walk around to the back of the big tent to give the signal to the performers who were all lined up there ready to go.

"Hold it, Barton," shouted Mr. Carlin, suddenly. "There's something coming around the bend in the road."

There was a gay hubbub of voices from a crowd of some sort coming around the bend. In a few minutes Mr. Barton and Mr. Carlin could see them clearly. It was a big crowd of children. Actually, all the boys and girls of Tannersville, all hopping, skipping and running and all of them talking and laughing at the same time. And in the center of the group surrounded on all sides by the boys and girls of Tannersville was . . .

"BO!" . . . IT'S BO!" shouted Mr. Carlin. "Hey, Barton! Hey, Danny! Bo's come back and he brought his own audience! All the boys and girls!"

The men at the ticket windows worked as quickly as they could getting out tickets for the boys and girls. In a few minutes a crowd of them tramped into the tent, climbed up on the wooden seats and were ready for the big show to begin.

Meanwhile, Danny with a welcoming arm wrapped around Bo's trunk led him around to the back of the tent so that he would be in his proper place in the Grand Parade.

"Oh, boy, am I glad to see you again, Bo," said Danny as he happily led Bo to the back of the tent. "Where have you been, boy? How'd you get back?"

Naturally Bo said nothing. But he looked just as happy as Danny. What really happened was this. In the farmer's cow pasture Bo had heard the sound of the steam calliope borne on the wind as the circus paraded through Tannersville. His sensitive big ears had heard the steam calliope's

mournful notes even though the cow pasture was some distance from the center of Tannersville.

Bo had walked directly across the fields, over the stone walls, across a creek, through a lumber yard, over the railroad tracks until he got to Tannersville's main street. By the time he got there the parade was over and everyone had gone home for lunch. But Bo picked up the trail of the Circus Parade. He saw the burst balloons that were dropped every now and then when some of the children had blown them up too high. He saw the empty popcorn and peanut bags and shells that people dropped along the curb as they watched the parade.

He saw too the spangles and bits of colored feathers that had dropped off the beautiful costumes worn by the ladies and gentlemen who rode the big handsome circus horses. And he saw too the cores of apples and now and then the pieces of carrots that were dropped as people fed the horses when the parade stood still.

So Bo followed the trail of the circus parade through and around Tannersville until he had followed it right back to the Big Meadows where the Big Tent was set up.

Naturally, as he walked along the streets of Tannersville, since there was no school (remember the half-holiday?), Bo now and then met a boy or girl. And naturally the children walked with him. Soon there was quite a

77

crowd of boys and girls walking along with him . . . And more kept coming . . . And they came right along to the circus with him!

Naturally, Bo couldn't tell that to anybody . . . But it really was the most natural thing in the world the way Bo, the red, white and blue elephant, lost the B. & C. Circus and found it again.

2:45 P.M. *The Show Goes On*

$\mathcal{B}$EFORE the Grand Parade started Danny did a quick patch-up job on Bo's paint work. So much of Bo's paint had been scraped off and washed off as he wandered around Tannersville in the early morning fog he looked rather faded. His red paint had become pink, his white became grey, and his blue . . . sort of a light blue, almost lavender. Danny quickly mixed three buckets of red, white and blue paint and he slapped some color on Bo's hide with a big brush. But the new color was much brighter than the old color. Now his paint was so spotty Bo looked like a calico-colored elephant!

But nothing could be done about it. The signal had been given and the Grand Parade began.

The Grand Parade around the arena was very spectacular. There were many wonderful clowns, acrobats and other performers in marvelous costumes. And there were animals with dazzlingly beautiful trappings. But the one who got the most applause, cheers and attention was one of the Red, White and Blue painted elephants, the one who looked more like a calico-colored elephant . . . the one named Bo.

There were quite a few people sitting in the audience

who seemed to see something familiar in the red, white and blue, calico-colored elephant. Miss Phoebe sitting in a seat down front with her older sister said into her sister's good ear, "That last elephant there . . . did you notice how much he looks like Mr. McCracken's old sorrel horse? Especially when he curls up his trunk."

And Mr. McCracken himself sitting some seats back said to his neighbors who happened to be a farmer and his wife, "Powerful fellers, those elephants. We sure could use their power in a railroad yard. I mean pushing freight cars along sidings and things like that."

The farmer nodded and said, "Yep . . . Yep, they're powerful fellers but I wouldn't want to have any of them around my farm. Seems like I saw that spotted one somewhere before."

The farmer's wife sniffed and said nothing.

A lot of second grade children were wildly excited when the elephants marched toward them in the Grand Parade. They stood up and called to their second grade teacher who was sitting with a group of other teachers near Mr. Mason, the principal, and his wife.

"Teacher!" shouted the second grade children. "Hey, teacher! Look . . . Pink Elephants!"

The embarrassed teacher waved them down but the children were up again when the elephants had passed.

"Teacher!" they screamed with delight. "Look, Blue Elephants!"

Mr. Mason chuckled as he leaned across and said to the second-grade teacher, "It does look as if there really are pink and blue elephants after all."

The physical education teacher said nothing about the elephants . . . even when later they tossed a ball back and forth dressed up as baseball players.

But Benny Lawrence had a lot to say real loud about elephants, especially about the one elephant he knew personally.

"There he is, Pop," he yelled at the top of his lungs, "the last one. That's the one I saw. Yes sir, I saw him first before anybody. You see him, Pop? . . . The last red, white and blue elephant. . . ."

"All right, Benny, all right," said his father. "All right, so you saw the last elephant first."

The only one who had anything to do with Bo when he wandered through and around Tannersville who did not see him at the circus was the man who drove the steam shovel. He had work to do. He had to go on digging the big hole deeper . . . alone. He had no audience watching him. Everybody was at the circus. And it was too bad (for his sake) because he missed a marvelous show.

After all the other wonderful circus acts were finished and after the chariot race was run, Mr. Carlin, wearing the regular uniform of a ringmaster, complete with silk top hat and scarlet tailcoat, walked out to the center of the big ring. He blew his whistle, raised his hands high in the air. The two circus bands stopped playing and everybody stopped laughing and talking.

"La-d-ies . . . and Gen-tle-men . . . Your attention please!" shouted Mr. Carlin. "Ladies and gentlemen . . . it now gives me great pleasure to present . . . our Stupendous, Colossal, Magnificent Grand Finale act . . . Presenting for the first time under any tent the most astound-

ing Animal Act in the World . . . the Red, White and
Blue Elephant Triplets . . . JO . . . UM . . . and last but
not least BO!"

The bands played a fanfare as all the spotlights in the
tent were thrown at the performers' entrance at the end
of the arena. Both bands together blared out with the
music of "The Red, White and Blue." Then out into the
milky white glare of the spotlights marched Jo, Um and
Bo walking on their hind legs and waving high in the air
in the tips of their trunks small American flags!

It was so astounding and beautiful a sight the audience
gasped, then they burst out with cheers and wild applause!

Jo, Um and Bo marched right out into the center of the
big ring in a blaze of spotlights. There they gave Danny

their little American Flags. Then as the music changed
to the "Blue Danube" they whirled neatly through a slow,
dreamy waltz and followed that with a rather quick Cuban
dance. The Cuban dance is called the Conga.

The last of their three dances was most amazing. Some
roustabouts helped Danny strap three gigantic ruffled
skirts sprinkled with silver spangles around Jo, Um and
Bo's waists. This time in a delicate blue spotlight to the
music of "Glow little Glow-worm" they danced as dainty
a Ballet as anyone ever saw. Up on their tiptoes!

Their act went on with a baseball game (in costume),
then a comic bit, when Jo, dressed up as a mother, and
Um, dressed up as a father, pushed a baby carriage as big

as a truck that held Bo dressed up as a baby . . . and the act ended after Mr. Carlin's announcement that Jo, Um and Bo would do the greatest trick ever seen in circus history . . . both here and abroad!

While Jo, Um and Bo had been going through their act the roustabouts had been very busy in the shadows outside of the spotlights. Suddenly the spotlights were switched over to reveal what the roustabouts had been doing. They had erected a narrow steel beam about twenty feet long and about ten feet off the ground. At each end of the beam there were two big ramps. After a roll of drums the bands played "When Johnny Comes Marching Home."

Jo, Um and Bo, one by one, walked up the ramp at one end of the steel beam and when they got up to the beam they each in turn stood up on their front legs with their hind quarters high in the air (just like Bo had done at the second grade window) and they walked across the narrow steel beam! That was the trick!

Carefully placing one big foot in front of the other Jo crossed the beam first. He was followed by Um. Then it came Bo's turn to cross the narrow beam.

Bo carefully walked across until he came to the middle of the beam. There to everyone's surprise he wavered and stopped! Then Bo rested his curled up trunk on the narrow

beam and very slowly and deliberately lifted his left front foot off the beam! And then . . . (as everyone gasped) he lifted his right front foot off the beam!

Bo balanced himself . . . his whole weight . . . on that narrow beam just on his curled up *nose!* (so to speak, since elephants' trunks are really their noses).

Neither his front feet nor his back feet touched the steel beam. No hands! No feet! And Bo held himself up on his curled up nose (or trunk) for TEN WHOLE SECONDS!

The band stopped playing! Everyone stopped talking and laughing and *breathing* for those long ten seconds! The silence in that circus tent full of people was so intense it almost hurt the ear drums!

At last (to everyone's relief) Bo calmly brought his left front foot back to the beam . . . then his right front foot . . . and he lifted his trunk! And then, with modest dignity, Bo crossed the beam and went down the ramp still walking on his front legs with his hind quarters high in the air!

The applause was thunderous!

The Grand Finale Act was done!

"What a performance!" shouted Mr. Carlin into Danny's ear above the sound of the music and the roars of the delighted audience. "Who taught Bo to do that new trick?"

Danny with a grin that just about slit his face in half shook his head. He didn't know. He cupped his hands and shouted, "Guess he just wanted to do something special for the boys and girls."

The music blared even louder playing over and over again "When Johnny Comes Marching Home." In the excitement the bands had forgotten that Jo, Um and Bo's exit music was the same as their entrance music, "Three cheers for the Red, White and Blue," and they played "When Johnny Comes Marching Home" over and over again.

Jo, Um and Bo were called back to take bow after bow!

And in the excitement Mr. Carlin found himself singing out loud with the bands. But he was not singing the words "When Johnny Comes Marching Home." He was singing "When Bo Comes Marching Home!"

"Danny," he shouted, "I've got a new song!" and he ran to the center of the arena blowing his whistle as he ran.

The music stopped and the people quieted down to hear Mr. Carlin as he bellowed to the crowd.

"Ladies and gentlemen! I'd like to have you join me with new words to an old song that I just made up! . . . Please sing along with me! . . . Here it is!"

He gave a signal to the band to again play the music for "When Johnny Comes Marching Home."

Then Mr. Carlin roared out his new words to that old song. After the second line everybody was singing with him because Mr. Carlin's new words were not too different from the old words of the song:

"When *Bo* comes marching home again, Hur-rah, Hur-rah!
We'll give him a hearty welcome then, Hur-rah, Hur-rah!
The men will cheer, the boys will shout
The girls and ladies will all turn out
And we'll all feel gay when *Bo* comes marching home."

And to the sound of Mr. Carlin, Danny Morgan and all the people in the circus tent singing . . . and both circus bands and the steam calliope playing "When Bo Comes Marching Home" . . . the Grand Finale Act ended! And the Big Show ended! And the most Stupendous, the most Colossal, the most Magnificent, April First in the history of Tannersville . . . the day when Bo and the circus came to town . . . ENDED!

THE END